The Newspaper Kids 1

Blue Rock Kid Power

First published in Australia by **Angus&Robertson** in 1996
An imprint of HarperCollins*Publishers*, Australia
First published in Great Britain by Collins 1999
Collins is an imprint of HarperCollins*Publishers* Ltd,
77-85 Fulham Palace Road, Hammersmith, London W6 8JB

The HarperCollins website address is www.**fire**and**water**.com

3 5 7 9 8 6 4 2

Text copyright © Juanita Phillips 1996

ISBN 0 00 675460 0

The author asserts the moral right to be identified as author of the work

Printed and bound in Great Britain by
Omnia Books Limited, Glasgow

Conditions of Sale
This book is sold subject to the condition that it shall not, by way of
trade or otherwise, be lent, re-sold, hired out or otherwise circulated,
without the publisher's prior consent in any form, binding or cover
other than that in which is it published and without a similar condition
including this condition being imposed on the subsequent purchaser.

The Newspaper Kids 1

Blue Rock Kid Power

Juanita Phillips

Illustrations by Mark David

Collins

An Imprint of HarperCollinsPublishers

Meet... The Newspaper Kids

Hugo Lilley

Jasper and I are so close in age we are almost twins but, unlike me, my older sister can be a pain — she's always grabbing the good things for herself. So when it came to giving ourselves jobs on our newspaper, no one was more surprised than me to be given the job of chief reporter.

Chasing criminals and solving mysteries was what I'd always wanted to do, but chief reporter? That sounded important . . . and, what's even better, fun!

Jasper Lilley

Thank goodness, Hugo agreed to be chief reporter because while he's chasing criminals, someone has to interview the famous people . . . and that leaves me! It won't be easy — being glamorous is hard work. Most importantly, the kids of Blue Rock need a voice and mine's the loudest.

Everyone has a right to be heard; especially kids, and especially me!

Toby Trotter

Putting together a newspaper is a bit like putting together a jigsaw. And to put together a good newspaper, you need a lot of pieces.

That's why I am lucky to have the help of my best friend, Jasper and her brother, Hugo. What Jasper doesn't know, Hugo is certain to find out!

**If a story breaks . . .
the newspaper kids are
on the case!**

For Gaby, just because she's special — J. P.

Chapter One

It all started the day I had my big accident on the skate ramp.

One minute it was my turn for the skates and I was hooting up the side of the ramp like a real speed demon, ready to do one of my brilliant turns and come back down again. The next minute . . .

CLUNK! That was my big sister Jasper, sticking out one of her long bony legs and tripping me up.

WHOOSH! That was me, doing a fantastic freefall, minus the parachute.

SPLAT! That was also me, hitting the ground beside the skate ramp with a great big bellyflop. Then I blacked out.

The next thing I knew, Jasper was bawling and blubbering over the top of me, and I was eating dirt pie.

'Don't die, Hugo,' she bellowed. 'Help! Hugo's dead!' Jasper threw her arms around me and sobbed into my ear. 'Please don't be dead, Hugo. I'm sorry I tripped you. From now on, you can have first go on the skates whenever you want.'

I kept my eyes shut and acted like a corpse. If old Bossy Boots was making offers like that, I was happy to listen.

'You can *have* them,' she sobbed. 'Take the skates. Just don't die.'

I opened one eye just in time to see help arriving.

'Thanks, sis,' I croaked weakly. 'I'll hold you to that.'

I didn't get to keep the skates. Mum and Dad said we still had to share them. They said there was a name for pretending to be dead when you aren't . . . fraud. Grown-ups go to jail for it.

Me, I was a prisoner in my own bed and that was no fun at all. Even having Jasper as my own personal slave was boring after a while.

'You could have killed me,' I reminded her. 'Now, go and get me some more of that hazelnut chocolate Mum hides in the fridge. Then I want you to play

Chinese chequers with me. And don't forget . . . you have to lose.'

Jasper did it, but I could tell she was getting grumpy.

'It's hard to lose against you, Hugo,' she complained later on. 'You're such a rotten player.'

My slave was getting restless and I knew that any minute she was going to turn back into a bossy big sister. Luckily, Mum came in just before she did.

'Well! This is a nice change to see you two getting on so well,' she said. 'Why can't you be like this all the time?'

Jasper gave Mum one of her big suck-up smiles. She was in the bad books big-time for nearly killing me.

'I just want Hugo to get better as quickly as possible Mum, so we can go back to the park.'

Jasper wasn't allowed to go to the park on her own, and neither was I. It had to be the two of us, for better or worse.

'Yeah, Mum! When can I get up? We've finished building this great tree house, and if we don't get back to it, that big bully Howard Fitzherbert's going to take it!'

Mum didn't answer straightaway. She sat down on the bed looking sad. It was just like the time she told us our dog Buster had been run over by a car. Suddenly, I felt scared.

'I've got some bad news for you,' Mum said. 'Dad's just called me on his mobile phone. The park is being closed. You can't go back.'

'What!' Jasper and I looked at each other, horrified.

'Because of Hugo's accident, people are saying it's too dangerous,' Mum explained. 'The skateboard ramp is old, the whole place is overgrown with weeds, and the council doesn't have enough money to fix it all.'

'But where will we play? There's nowhere else . . . and our tree house . . .' Jasper sounded like she was going to cry.

Mum sighed. 'I know it's hard, Jasper. But it's for your own good. And you can always play in the backyard.'

The backyard was okay, but we both knew it wasn't the same. There was no skate ramp. No big old fig tree with a tree house hidden among its giant branches. No creek with tadpoles in it. It was a disaster — our only playground was being taken away from us, and there was nothing we could do about it.

Or . . . was there? When Mum left the room, Jasper and I looked at each other. We're not twins — I'm ten and she's eleven — but sometimes, we can read each other's mind.

'Come on, Jas,' I said, leaping out of bed. 'Turn on the computer. Let's get a message to Toby. We've got work to do.'

The park was smack-bang in the middle of Blue Rock. Just about every street in town ran off it, including ours — Tumblegum Street. In fact, it was spooky. Pick a street — any street — and no matter what direction you headed in, you always ended up at the park. It drove tourists crazy.

'Back in the old days we called it the Village Green,' our Great-aunt Miranda told us. 'Every Saturday there were markets there, where everyone bought their fruit and vegies. In summer, there were bush dances and barbecues. Why, I even got married there.'

Great-aunt Miranda was at least a million years old and it was hard to imagine her being married to anyone, unless it was a caveman.

'My, how times have changed,' she sighed, her wrinkly old face looking sad. 'All the grown ups rushing around, too busy working to sit and have a chat with their neighbours. Buying their vegetables out of that big freezer at the Megamart. And the Village Green going to rack and ruin. It's a crying shame.'

It was even harder to imagine the park the way Great-aunt Miranda described it. These days the park was full of weeds and rusting car wrecks and we kids were the only ones who ever went there. It was ours. And now the council wanted to close it!

'Emergency! Meet us for a private discussion at the fig tree, now!'

That was the message we sent Toby Trotter. Toby was Jasper's best friend and he was seriously smart. He was so smart he'd hooked up our computers so we could send each other electronic mail. It was like our own private phone line, except nobody could listen in. Even better, we could send each other messages late at night when our parents thought we were in bed asleep.

If anyone could come up with a smart idea to stop the park being closed, it was Toby.

Quiet as mice, we snuck out of the house. We didn't want anybody to know where we were going. Mum was on the phone to Great-aunt Miranda. Good. She'd be yakking for hours.

Luckily, the street was deserted. The only person who saw us was Frankie Halliday. She was sitting on the front steps of her house, combing her long-haired cat.

'Oh, no,' groaned Jasper. 'I hope she doesn't follow us. Come on, let's hurry.'

'She's all right,' I said uncomfortably. 'Maybe we should ask her . . .'

'NOT!' Jasper charged ahead so fast I had to run to keep up with her.

I liked Frankie, but Jasper didn't. It was one of those things we didn't agree on. Frankie's dad had been a famous photographer who died in a car crash. Now she and her mum lived on their own.

When I turned around a few minutes later, Frankie was still sitting there quietly, stroking her cat and watching us.

By the time we got to the park, Toby was already there. And so, for some reason, were lots of other people. So much for our private discussion.

'I got your message . . . what's up?' asked Toby. 'Why are all these people here?'

'Search me,' said Jasper. 'Look, Toby, there's your dad!'

Mr Trotter was a reporter for the local newspaper, the *Blue Rock Bugle*, and it looked like he was here on duty.

'Hey! That's Marilyn Miller from Channel Five News,' continued Jasper excitedly. She's a bit starstruck, my sister. 'It must be a big story!' she added.

Just then, somebody started talking through a megaphone. It was Mayor Fitzherbert, Howard's dad. He has a big red face and flaps of skin hanging down from his cheeks like a bulldog. The crowd fell silent.

'Friends! Citizens of Blue Rock! This is a great day for our town!' Mayor Fitzherbert looked very pleased with himself.

'For years this vacant lot has been an eyesore. A blot on the beauty of our town! A DANGEROUS blot!' he thundered.

'Who's that standing next to the Mayor?' I whispered.

'That's Barry Plunder,' Jasper whispered back, 'from Plunder and Pillage. The big developer.'

The Mayor's red face was shining and his jowls were trembling with excitement. 'Fellow citizens, this vacant lot, this wasteland, is about to be transformed.'

Wasteland? Vacant lot? The Mayor was talking about our park!

'Transformed, friends, into a paradise we can all be proud of. A paradise created by one of our finest businessmen, Mr Barry Plunder.'

Mr Plunder stepped forward with a big greasy grin and waved. His podgy hand was covered in gold rings.

'This,' murmured Toby, 'is very suspicious.'

'And friends, if you have any doubt, let me remind you,' the Mayor continued, 'this park is a danger to our children. Only yesterday, a child was almost killed when part of that old skate ramp collapsed. He fell right through it and almost cracked his skull open.'

Jasper gave me a sharp poke in the ribs that made me jump. 'Hey Bozo! He's talking about you.'

A concerned murmur ran through the crowd. People were nodding their heads. It looked like the Mayor had them convinced.

But it wasn't true! The ramp hadn't collapsed. I had to do something before it was too late — before the park was closed forever.

I took a deep breath, pushed my way to the front of the crowd, and said as loudly as I could: 'I didn't fall, Mayor Fitzherbert. My sister pushed me. Ladies and gentlemen . . . THE PARK IS SAFE!'

Chapter Two

Yikes! What was I doing in front of all these people?

Everyone was staring at me. The Mayor put down his megaphone. Jasper's mouth dropped open so hard her eyeballs nearly popped out. Behind his thick spectacles, I could see Toby blinking in surprise.

Suddenly this didn't seem like such a good idea. I crossed my fingers and tried to make myself invisible through sheer mind power. Nothing happened.

'Hey! Who's the boy with the bandage around his head?' Marilyn Miller, the TV reporter with yellow hair, fierce black eyebrows and giant shoulder pads, pushed her way to the front.

'Hugo Lilley,' said Toby's dad. 'Hugo, what are you doing here? You should be in bed.'

'Is that the boy who had the accident?' asked another reporter.

Within two seconds I was surrounded by them. Somebody shoved a TV camera in my face, then a big furry microphone. A radio reporter was trying to push in, waving her tape recorder in the air. All around me, people were shouting out, asking questions.

'You're on the air, boy,' someone said. 'Speak up.'

The Mayor gave me a dirty look but there wasn't a lot he could do. And anyway, I was starting to enjoy it.

'Yes, I'm the boy who fell off the skate ramp,' I said grandly.

A familiar voice interrupted. 'And I'm his sister. I'm responsible for the accident.'

Trust Jasper! Pushing in and trying to steal all th glory! I glared at her, but she was too busy prin and preening in front of the TV camera to no

'On behalf of all the children of Blu don't want the park to close,' Jas importantly. 'Even though it's ru it's perfectly safe. And there' to play.'

The TV crew was try Jasper's face, but she kept

her best side. I didn't have the heart to tell her all they were getting was a close-up of her ear.

'Jasper's right,' I said. 'The Mayor says we should build something else here, but he's wrong! It's our park and we love it.'

I could see Toby giving me the thumbs-up sign. Great! I was saying all the right things. But just as I was warming up, Mayor Fitzherbert had to barge right in and spoil it all.

'Come along everyone,' he said smoothly. 'These young people have had their say, and now it's time for them to go off and do their homework.'

'It's school holidays, Mayor,' said Jasper. 'We don't have any homework.'

'Ha, ha! I like a girl who speaks her mind,' said the Mayor, looking like he wanted to kill her. 'Run along now. We've got important things to talk about. Far too important for you to be wasting our time.'

'But I haven't finished,' I squawked. 'I'm just getting started.'

The Mayor didn't even hear me. He was too busy erding the reporters away.

'Only kids,' I heard him say with a forced chuckle. cky we know what's best for them, hey?'

hed home to turn the TV news on.

Toby,' said Mum, walking into the lounge

room. Then she saw me. Gulp. 'Hugo! What are you doing out of bed?'

We didn't give her time to be mad.

'Guess what, Mum? We're famous! We're going to be on the news! We saved the park!' Jasper and I were talking over the top of each other with excitement.

Mum was so surprised she forgot to be angry. In fact, she rang Dad and told him to hurry home to see us on the news. Then she rang Mr Trotter and invited him too.

'You'll be on TV too, won't you Toby?'

Toby blushed bright red and blinked very hard behind his glasses. 'No way, Mrs Lilley,' he said modestly. 'I'm just behind the scenes.'

'Well, I'm sure Hugo and Jasper couldn't have done it without you. And it's about time we saw your father again. He spends far too much time on his own.'

Dad and Mr Trotter made it home in record time.

'I've got butterflies,' I whispered to Jasper. 'Imagine how many people are going to see us on TV. Thousands! Maybe millions!'

Jasper had a dreamy, faraway look on her face. 'Maybe I'll be discovered,' she said. 'I've always wanted to be a movie star. Toby, do you think they filmed my best side?'

Toby thought carefully. 'No. But they got a good shot of your ear.'

'Quiet everyone,' said Dad. 'The news is starting.'

'The Mayor of Blue Rock made an exciting announcement today,' said the newsreader. 'Here's Marilyn Miller with the details.'

Marilyn Miller! That was the lady with the gridiron shoulder pads who'd asked me questions. Any minute now, we'd be on.

Marilyn Miller's voice took over. 'More than a hundred residents turned out today to hear the council's plans,' she said.

Pictures of the crowd flashed onto the screen.

'Hey, there's me!' Mr Trotter jumped out of his chair and pointed wildly at a speck on the TV.

'Sit down, Dad,' said Toby calmly. 'Control yourself.'

Then the Mayor came on, talking about the park being closed so it could be turned into a paradise. His big red face filled the whole screen.

'What about us?' said Jasper impatiently. 'Come on Marilyn, you're running out of time.'

Marilyn appeared on the screen, holding a microphone and looking very serious. 'Even the local children say it's a good idea,' she said.

'No we don't,' I protested. 'Marilyn's got it wrong.'

Suddenly Jasper screamed. 'Oh, look, it's me! I'm on television!'

'Settle down,' ordered Dad. 'We want to hear what you're saying.'

There was a close-up of Jasper's ear, then her voice saying, 'It's run-down and untidy.'

'I didn't say that,' said Jasper, flustered. 'I'm sure I didn't.'

'Quiet! Hugo's on,' Dad said.

There I was. It was my big moment. Jasper hadn't performed too well, so it was up to me to save the day.

I saw my face on television staring straight back at me, and heard my voice saying, 'We should build something else here.'

'Hey!' I yelled angrily. 'She cut out the rest of what I said. I didn't mean that at all!'

The report finished with Marilyn Miller saying: 'So it seems that everyone agrees, the park must close. Marilyn Miller, Channel Five News.'

Dad turned the TV off. Nobody said a word. We were all too shocked.

'Well, kids, I think you've just learned a hard lesson,' said Dad finally.

Jasper said faintly: 'Really and truly, I didn't say that about the park. I said we wanted to keep it open.'

I nodded. 'The same with me. Marilyn Miller only used a tiny bit of what we said and made it sound like the complete opposite.'

Mr Trotter shook his head. 'It's not fair, but it happens all the time. In my business, you can twist people's words to mean anything you like.'

Toby piped up hopefully. 'What about your story, Dad? We've still got that. You wouldn't twist our words. People can read the paper tomorrow and get both sides of the story.'

He was right! We still had a chance.

'I'm sorry, son,' said Mr Trotter. 'I did put Hugo and Jasper in the story, but the editor took them out. He said nobody cares what kids think. I did argue with him, but . . .' He shrugged his shoulders helplessly.

So that was it. Our one big chance to save the park, and we'd blown it.

'Looks like you're not going to Hollywood, sis,' I said gloomily.

We were sitting in Jasper's room with the lights off, throwing balls of paper at her glow-in-the-dark skeleton.

'Well, I guess it's not that important,' sighed Jasper. 'I just wish there was some way we could get people to listen to us.'

I stared glumly at the skeleton. With its glowing green grin, it seemed to be laughing at us. And who could blame it? Mr Trotter was right. We were only kids. Who cared what we thought?

'It's so unfair.' I hurled my last bit of scrunched-up paper at the skeleton and missed by a mile. 'There are more kids than grown-ups in this neighbourhood. Imagine if we formed an army! Then they'd listen to us.'

'Yeah!' Jasper cheered up immediately. 'We could take them all prisoner and then do whatever we want. The first thing I'd do is sack Marilyn Miller and confiscate that big microphone she sticks in everyone's face.'

'You could swap places with her, and ask *her* the questions,' I suggested. 'Ask her why her hair is that funny yellow colour when her eyebrows are black.'

Jasper giggled. 'And you could take over the *Bugle*. Then we could write whatever we wanted to!'

'That'd teach the editor a lesson. I bet he . . .'

BEEP BEEP! It was the computer, with an incoming message. Our plans would have to wait.

'That'll be Toby,' I said, going over to have a look. 'Our one and only friend.'

'Yeah. Everyone else hates us now because they think we really meant those things on TV,' said Jasper forlornly.

'Look — Toby reckons he's got an idea.'

Toby's electronic mail message said:

> MAY HAVE SOLUTION TO OUR PROBLEM.

I typed back:

> RUNNING AWAY TO SIBERIA?
>
> ALREADY THOUGHT OF IT.

There was a pause, then:

> NO, REALLY. A WAY TO SAVE THE PARK.

Jasper and I looked at each other and shrugged. What on earth was Toby thinking of?

The computer beeped again:

> WE NEED TO LET PEOPLE KNOW THE REAL STORY.

I typed back impatiently:

> WE ALREADY KNOW THAT.
>
> STOP KEEPING US IN SUSPENSE.

The computer cursor blinked twice. Then, after what seemed an eternity, the most brilliant idea I'd ever heard of was sitting on the screen in front of us.

It said:

> LET'S START OUR OWN NEWSPAPER!

Chapter Three

To get to Toby's, you cut through old Mrs Stackett's backyard. It saved time, but you had to be careful she didn't spot you.

'Hey Hugo. When we start the newspaper, we can write a story about old Mr Stackett too,' Jasper whispered as we clambered across our fence into enemy territory. 'Mum says he's an invalid, but I bet Mrs Stackett's chained him to his wheelchair so he doesn't run away.'

'Or maybe he died years ago, and she keeps his body in the lounge room and talks to it . . . QUICK! Here she comes!'

We bolted through the hole in the fence just in

time. Old Mrs Stackett was at the back door, waving and calling out to us. Lucky for us she moved so slowly, or she might have caught us and taken us prisoner.

Toby was in the kitchen, cooking breakfast for his dad. When we walked in he was peering into a boiling saucepan.

'Poached eggs,' he announced, his glasses fogged up with steam. 'If you cook them too long, they go rubbery.'

Ever since Toby's mum left, Toby had cooked for him and his dad. Most of the recipes he got off the back of food packets — delicious things like chicken satays with peanut sauce and little pizzas with long stringy cheese that stuck to your teeth.

This time, though, he was cooking poached eggs with mushrooms and fried tomatoes.

'I'll take this into Dad and meet you in the Cave,' said Toby. 'The door's locked, but you know the combination. We can talk privately in there.'

The Cave was a tumbledown wooden shed, buried deep in the dark jungle of the Trotter's backyard. Once upon a time, it had been a garage. But now it was covered with ivy and almost hidden by trees.

As we walked towards it, I thought I saw a movement out of the corner of my eye. A flash of red among the trees. Was someone following us?

But when I looked, there was nobody there. I shivered. Just my imagination.

We dialled the secret combination on the padlock, then let ourselves in. Even though I'd been inside the Cave a million times before, it was always a surprise, like walking into another world.

This was Toby's special place — his secret hideaway. Nobody knew about it except us and his dad.

The guardian of the Cave was Toby's computer, Myron. Not only did Myron have a name, Myron had a printer to talk to and a special dust cover to keep him clean.

'Toby likes that computer more than he likes us,' grumbled Jasper.

Myron's cursor blinked underneath its plastic dust cover. It was like a green eye, watching us.

'Don't talk too loudly,' I told Jasper, 'Myron's listening!'

The rest of the place was shabby, but comfortable. The floor was covered with faded Persian rugs that Toby had collected from garage sales. To sit on, there were two fat old sofas with their insides spilling out. Someone had left them on the footpath during the big council clean-up, and the three of us had somehow managed to drag them all the way back to the Cave.

In the corner, there was a small fridge full of food supplies. During the holidays, Toby sometimes stayed in here for days at a time working at his computer and he always made sure he had plenty to eat and drink.

'If we ever got snowed in we could probably survive for six months in here,' I said, peeking inside the fridge. 'Look, Jasper — bread, tinned tuna, baked beans, tomato, some ham . . . he's even got some chocolate biscuits.'

'As if we'd be snowed in, dummy,' said Jasper. 'It doesn't snow in Australia. It's too hot.'

'So what's that white stuff that people ski on?' I retorted. 'Dandruff?'

'Break it up, you two.' It was Toby. He plonked himself in a chair in front of Myron and took off the dust cover. 'Let's get down to business. We've got to stop the park being closed and we don't have a lot of time to do it. By my calculations, we've got less than a week to get our own newspaper on the street so that people hear *our* side of the story.'

Toby typed in his password and Myron hummed into life. 'Okay. Ideas, anyone?'

Jasper and I looked at him blankly.

'I think we need some brain food,' I said. 'I'll open the chocolate biscuits.'

'What I want to know,' said Jasper, 'is how? I know

we want to stand up for kids' rights, but we don't know the first thing about writing our own newspaper.'

I nodded. She had a point.

'Well, as far as I can see, a newspaper is just a collection of stories.' Toby tossed a copy of the *Blue Rock Bugle* on his desk and took a biscuit. 'All of us are good at writing stories. We've got Myron. We've got a printer. We've even got a scanner so we can have photographs in it if we want. I don't see a problem.'

Toby made it all sound so easy. He jabbed at the front page of the *Bugle* with a chocolate-smeared finger. 'See that big headline? That's the main story. It takes up most of the front page. We'll do our own, of course, about the park.'

Jasper tugged at one of her orange plaits doubtfully. 'You can't just have one story. What else are we going to put in it?'

'Don't forget old Mrs Stackett's husband,' I reminded her. 'A dead body is worth writing about.'

'A dead body?' Toby sat up. 'Sounds like a good crime story.' If he'd had antennas, they would have been wiggling like rabbit's ears.

'It is but it's still not enough,' argued Jasper. 'You can't have a newspaper with just two stories in it. And nothing much ever happens around here anyway.'

'I disagree.' Toby flicked through the paper. 'This is a grown-ups' paper but we can get ideas from it.

Like the sport section. Kids play sport. We can write about that. And here's a gossip column . . .'

'Jasper could write that,' I said innocently. 'We could call it Big Mouth . . . OUCH!'

Toby ignored us. 'Here's another idea. Old Dr Dodd writes a weekly health report. We could do something like that as well.'

'But old Dr Dodd is so boring!' I objected. 'All he writes about is arthritis.'

Toby blinked at me impatiently. 'No, the idea is that we write our own health report. We could call it . . . let's see . . . Dr Death!'

I burst out laughing. Dr Death! 'We can have a photo of you dressed up in a white coat, Toby. With a stethoscope!'

Jasper clapped her hands in excitement. 'People could write and ask you for advice. Like, "Dear Dr Death, how can I break out in big red boils so I can stay home from school?"'

I was starting to see what Toby meant. Writing our own newspaper was serious business . . . but it could also be a lot of fun.

'Look, here's a section called the Social Pages,' said Jasper, breathless from laughing. 'It's about grown-ups going to parties.'

I looked over her shoulder. There was a whole page of photographs of people dressed up and looking silly.

'We could have our own social pages!' I handed around the chocolate biscuits again. 'Kids are always having birthday parties around here.'

'Exactly. And they're much more interesting than grown-up parties,' said Toby. 'Remember when Porky Merron let all of Mr Quinn's prize pigeons out of the aviary by mistake?'

Did I ever! Porky was so scared he ran away and ended up turning himself in at a police station on the other side of town when it got dark.

'He didn't realise they were homing pigeons,' I chuckled. 'They all flew back! The birds were in bed asleep before he was!'

'That's the sort of stuff we have to report,' Toby nodded. 'Anything that kids are talking about is news, as far as we're concerned. Everyone will want to read it. We might even make a lot of money if we sell enough copies.'

'Yeah!' I hadn't even thought of that. If we made some money, Jasper and I could afford to buy another pair of skates. Then another thought struck me. 'And I know heaps about newspapers, from my paper run.'

Jasper rolled her eyes. 'Delivering a paper is very different from *writing* one, Hugo. Next thing, you'll want to be the editor.'

Hmmm . . . that wasn't a bad idea. Except that what

I really wanted to be was a crime reporter. Being the editor sounded important but I knew I'd rather be out chasing criminals and solving mysteries.

'That's a point,' said Toby thoughtfully. 'We need an editor. Someone who's in charge of the whole thing. Checking the reporters' stories and putting headlines on them.'

'Someone smart,' I said.

'Someone who's cool and calm under pressure,' added Jasper.

We looked at each other, then we looked at Toby.

'YOU!' we both shouted at the same time.

Toby blinked, and looked embarrassed.

'You'd be perfect,' I said. 'You know all about newspapers because of your dad. And you know how to work Myron.'

'And after all, it *was* your idea,' added Jasper.

Old Bossy Boots was certainly in a generous mood. I was surprised she hadn't grabbed the best job for herself.

'Well, if you both think so . . .'

I could tell Toby was really rapt, because his face was bright red and he was blinking faster than ever.

'That's settled then,' said Jasper, taking charge as usual. 'Toby's the editor. Hugo, you can be the chief reporter.'

Chief reporter! It sounded good.

'As for me,' continued Jasper, looking pleased with herself. 'I'll be the photographer. I can use the little Nifti-snap camera I got for Christmas.'

Toby shot me a nervous sideways glance. He'd seen Jasper's photos. So had I. The people in them nearly always ended up without heads. Once she'd done a portrait of me, and the only bit she got in was my elbow and part of my foot. Jasper thought they were artistic.

'Well?' she demanded. 'I know it sounds glamorous, but from what I hear it's very hard work.'

'Er ... you're right. It is a pretty tough job, Jasper,' said Toby. 'Maybe you should be a reporter. We need as many as we can get.'

'What!' Jasper turned on us. 'And take orders from my little brother? If you think I'm going to do that, Toby Trotter, you've got rocks in your head. Besides, if I don't take photographs, who will?'

There was a long silence. I racked my brains for an answer.

'I will,' said a voice.

The three of us spun around. There, standing in the doorway wearing a bright red shirt, was Frankie Halliday.

'How did you find us?' demanded Jasper. 'This is private. Nobody's allowed in here except us.'

Frankie blushed. 'I only wanted to talk to Hugo. I couldn't help overhearing about the newspaper. I'd love to help.'

She took a deep breath and looked Jasper right in the eye. 'I've got all my dad's old cameras. He . . . he taught me how to use them. Before . . . before the accident.'

I thought I heard Frankie's voice trembling, but Jasper didn't seem to notice. When Barracuda Brain makes up her mind, that's that.

'Sorry,' said Jasper coldly. 'We've already decided. I'm the photographer and I've got a perfectly good instamatic.'

I pulled Jasper aside. 'Maybe we should give her a go,' I whispered. 'She's really good. You know she won first prize in the school photography competition.'

It was the wrong thing to say. Too late, I remembered that Jasper had also entered the competition. Her headless portrait of Miss Finch the teacher didn't even get a Highly Commended.

Jasper glared at me. 'Are you crazy? She's got a stupid name and I don't like the way she's always hanging around,' she whispered back. 'What does she want anyway? She knows we're a trio. Why doesn't she make her own friends instead of trying to push in on us?'

She turned to Frankie and shook her head.

'Thanks, but no thanks,' she snapped. 'We don't want your help. See you later, Frankie.'

Frankie's dark eyes flashed. It was a look I'd never seen before, and I couldn't work it out.

'I'll show you,' she said.

And then she was gone.

Chapter Four

Word spread fast. By the time we held our first official meeting the next day, every kid in town knew about our newspaper. Not only that, they all wanted to help.

'Well, we're public property now,' sighed Toby. He was up a ladder, busy hammering a sign that said, 'Newspaper Office' above the door of the Cave. 'No point trying to keep this place a secret anymore. At least people know we're in business.'

Inside, I stuck a big piece of butcher's paper on the wall and wrote 'Story List' in thick felt pen at the top. That was so we could keep track of what stories we were covering, and who was writing them. Underneath, in smaller letters, I wrote 'Park Closing', with my name next to it. At least we had one good story to investigate. Now, we just had to fill the rest of the butcher's paper with story ideas.

Meanwhile Jasper kept the sightseers away. She was good at that — half human, half guard-dog.

'Are you just here for a sticky-beak or do you have a news tip for us?' she asked everyone who turned up. 'Just a sticky-beak? Well, off you go then.'

But for every time-waster, there was someone with a good story.

'I never realised so much happened around here,' said Jasper. 'Did you know the new people in Number 24 belong to a nudist club? Darcy Drayton reckons they walk around the house with no clothes on.'

'How would he know?' Darcy was in my class at school and I knew he was a bit of a liar.

'He looked through the window,' replied Jasper, checking her notes. 'But I said we couldn't do anything without proof. I might take my camera around later on.'

'Hang on!' said Toby, alarmed. 'You can get arrested for taking those sort of pictures.'

'Oh? Well, that's no good, then. But how about this one?' Jasper flicked through the maths pad she was using as a notebook. 'Now, where was it?

Ah, here we are . . . Kylie Fletcher's dog has had puppies.'

'That's old news,' I said. 'Everyone already knows that.'

'Yes, but one of them only has three legs,' said Jasper enthusiastically. 'If they don't find an owner for it, they'll have to put it to sleep.'

Toby nodded. 'We could have a public appeal. We could call it "Save the three-legged dog appeal".'

Toby added 'Three-legged Dog' to the story list. 'Jasper, we'll need a photograph. And make sure you get all three legs in, please.'

'Otherwise, it'll be the two-legged, headless dog appeal,' I snickered. Jasper threw a pencil at me. 'Ouch! That was sharp!'

Just then, there was another knock at the door.

'Are you here for a sticky-beak or . . .' started Jasper.

'No, we've got a news tip.' It was the Quinn twins, speaking in unison.

'Fire away,' said Toby.

'Well, it's like this —' said one twin.

'We want to get our ears pierced —' said the other.

'And Mum and Dad are being really mean about it —' continued Quinn Twin One.

'And they won't let us!' finished Quinn Twin Two.

'Stop, stop!' Toby held his hand up. 'I know you two think alike, but this is ridiculous. Which one are you?' He pointed at Twin One.

'I'm Jackie.'

'And I'm Julie,' said the other one.

'Okay. Jackie — you tell the story. Julie — try not to finish her sentences for her.'

The twins nodded agreement.

'The thing is, Mum and Dad say we have to wait until we're twelve to get our ears pierced,' said Jackie. 'But that's not for another two years. And all the girls in our class have had their ears pierced already.'

'It does sound like they're living in the Dark Ages,' agreed Jasper. 'After all, it's not as though you want a nose-ring or a stud in your bellybutton.'

'Exactly!' said Jackie eagerly. 'We heard your newspaper was going to stand up for kids' rights, so we thought you could help us.'

Toby was listening closely. 'It sounds like a good story,' he said. 'Another example of grown-ups not listening to what we think. It would be even better if you had some sort of protest. How about a hunger strike?'

The twins looked at each other doubtfully. 'We'd get into terrible trouble if we didn't eat our dinner,' said Jackie. 'And wouldn't we get awfully hungry?'

'That's the whole point of a hunger strike,' said Jasper impatiently. 'Look, you don't have to starve to death. Instead of going home for lunch one day, you sit outside with a sign. Your mum and dad'll soon give in. Just don't forget to tell us when you do it.'

The girls went home to work on their protest sign, while we wrote 'Twins Hunger Strike' on the story list. The butcher's paper was filling up fast and still the ideas kept coming.

'While Hugo's writing about the park, I'm going to investigate what old Mrs Stackett's done with her husband,' declared Jasper. 'If she's holding him prisoner, I'll take the pictures to prove it.'

'Just be careful you don't get caught,' warned Toby, writing it on the story list. 'Now, how about our notebooks and pens . . . Hugo, have you organised anything?'

'Have I ever!' As well as being chief reporter, I was also in charge of supplies. 'We don't have any money to spare, so this was the best I could do.'

'Hey, these aren't bad, little bro,' said Jasper admiringly as I handed out the notebooks. 'How did you make them?'

'Dad's old computer print-outs. I got them out of the recycling bin. They've only got writing on one side — so I turned them over, cut them into squares and stapled them together.'

'Great idea,' nodded Toby. 'How about the pens?'

'Elementary, my dear Trotter. When was the last time you cleaned out your school bag?'

Toby shrugged. 'Probably a year ago.'

'Errggh, disgusting!' Jasper wrinkled her nose. 'No wonder it stinks.'

'Well, you'd be amazed at what you'd find at the bottom of it,' I said, ignoring her. 'Including pens — millions of them. I guarantee every pen you've ever lost is lying at the bottom of your school bag. It's like a Black Hole.'

We were so busy planning the newspaper we didn't even hear the door to the Cave open.

Suddenly, there was the world's biggest show-off — mean, nasty Howard Fitzherbert. He was the son of the Mayor and the school's biggest bully.

'So!' Howard smirked. 'This is the big newspaper office, is it?'

'Rack off, drop-kick!' snapped Jasper. 'Who invited you?'

Howard grinned. 'Just interested. I can't believe you're using such a crummy old computer to write a newspaper on. It looks like something out of the Stone Age.'

I could feel my hands clenching with rage. Howard had the best computer in town and he made sure everybody knew it. The funny thing was, that no matter how much extra tutoring his dad paid for, Howard had never once beaten Toby in the Advanced Computers course at school. He always came in second. Not that you'd guess it by the way he acted.

He strolled over to Toby. 'My computer is much better than yours, Four-eyes.'

Toby nodded thoughtfully. 'That's true, Howard. But I can always exchange my computer for a better one. Unfortunately, you can't exchange brains. You're stuck with the one you've got.'

I hooted with laughter. Good old Trotter!

Howard's eyes narrowed into mean little slits. He looked at Toby. 'Very funny. We'll see who's laughing when nobody buys your stupid newspaper,' he said scornfully. 'And don't even try to get an interview with my father. He only talks to *real* reporters.'

'We are *real* reporters,' I said hotly. 'And we'll prove it by writing the *real* story about the park closing.'

Howard pounced like a rat on a piece of cheese. 'Oh, ho! So that's your big scoop,' he crowed. 'I suppose you think you can convince people to keep the old dump open.'

I could have kicked myself for telling him — and judging by the look on Jasper's face, so could she.

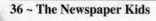

Howard's eyes glittered. For a split second he looked almost evil.

'I'm warning you,' he said. 'My father is the most important man in town. If you try and cross him — you'll regret it.'

He stood up and sauntered towards the door. 'By the way, do you have a name for this so-called newspaper of yours?'

We looked at each other blankly. The fact was, we hadn't even thought about it.

'I thought not,' grinned Howard. 'See you later, losers.'

Boy, so much for winning back our popularity. We'd made two enemies in two days, and we hadn't even written our first story.

Chapter Five

We soon forgot about the threats made by Howard and Frankie. There simply wasn't any time to worry about them. Apart from eating and sleeping, we spent every second of the next day organising the newspaper.

Toby decided we should have something called a 'Community Billboard' — little snippets of information about the people who lived in the neighbourhood.

'I don't care how trivial you think it is, I want to know about it,' he told us. 'Who's moving into Blue Rock, who's moving away, whose dogs got taken to the pound — weddings, babies, funerals, you name it. If kids are talking about it, we'll publish it.'

'That's a lot of work,' grumbled Jasper. 'How are we going to get the time for the really important stories?'

Toby furrowed his brow, thinking. 'Well, it seems like every kid in town wants to work for this newspaper, so why don't we take them up on it?'

'What, make them write the stories for us?' I asked.

'Sure. It's only the small stuff and it means less work for us.' Toby jumped to his feet, excited. 'Most families have got computers, so we'll just tell the kids to write their little bits of news on disk and drop it off here at the office. That way I can transfer it straight onto Myron!'

It was a brilliant idea and word spread like magic. By the next day we were up to our eyeballs in computer disks.

'At this rate, every family in town's going to get a mention,' I said, sorting through the latest arrivals. 'Hey, look at this one! Porky Merron says they've just found out what that terrible smell in their kitchen is. They looked everywhere, then they finally followed the smell right to the toaster — and guess what they found?'

'What?' Jasper asked.

'A dead mouse! Squashed flat in the crumb tray! It had been there for weeks!'

'Oh, gag.' Jasper pretended to put her finger down her throat. 'And they'd been eating toast all that time? That's a terrible story. It'll make people sick.'

'Precisely! That's why it's a *great* story,' Toby corrected her. 'Put it in the "yes" pile, Hugo. Then the two of you had better get cracking on your own stories. I'll start laying out the newspaper. We've got enough stories now to get started. I just have to figure out what page they'll go on, and where. Oh, and where to put your photographs, Jasper.'

'Making a newspaper is kind of like making a patchwork quilt,' said Jasper. 'Have you thought of a name yet?'

Toby shook his head. 'We can do that later. The most important thing is to write our stories. Especially you, Hugo. We need to save the park before the council decides to put something else there.'

I nodded. 'I know. We've got a tight deadline.'

Jasper looked sideways at me. 'What on earth does that mean?'

'It means we don't have a lot of time,' I explained patiently, as if she was a bit thick, even though I'd only just found out myself.

'Oh, you mean a *deadline*,' said Jasper breezily. 'Of course. I knew that. I just didn't hear you properly.'

'Now, have you got your camera, Jasper?' Toby said.

'Check.'

'Film?'

Jasper sighed impatiently. 'CHECK, Toby. As if I'd forget to put film in it. I'm a professional, remember.'

'Okay, okay, keep your hair on. I just wanted to make sure. Have you both got your notebooks and pens?'

'Check,' we said together.

'Good. Now, before we go our separate ways, there's only one thing left to do.'

Toby held out his hand, palm down. 'Make a tower.'

Jasper put her hand on top of Toby's and I put mine on top of hers. Then we added our other hands until we had a Friendship Tower. It was our own special ritual that we only used for very important occasions.

'Repeat after me,' said Toby, 'I swear to seek the truth and when I find it, to tell it without fear or favour.'

'I swear to seek the truth, and when I find it, to tell it without fear or favour,' we murmured.

'That is our solemn pledge,' said Toby.

'That is our solemn pledge.'

We looked at each other gravely. Making an oath on a Friendship Tower was serious stuff. It was a promise you couldn't break . . . ever.

Toby grinned.

'Well, what are you waiting for? Go the newspaper kids!'

Without fear or favour . . . I was still repeating the oath to myself, trying to figure out what it meant, as I backtracked home to get some food supplies. Toby was staying in the Cave to work on the newspaper. I had no idea where Jasper had disappeared to.

My plan was to head straight for the park to do some serious thinking about my story. I could sit in the tree house all day and work out a plan of attack without being bothered.

In the kitchen, I quickly loaded up my small day-pack with some muesli bars, cheese sandwiches and a carton of frozen pineapple juice. It was Sunday, so Mum and Dad wouldn't be too surprised if I didn't turn up for lunch. All the same, I didn't want them asking any questions about where I was heading. The park was now out of bounds, so the less they knew, the better.

Stuffing my notebook and pen into my day-pack, I bolted for the garage and put on the skates. 'First in, best dressed,' I murmured to myself as I strapped on the knee pads and wrist guards. Jasper would have to use the bike.

I sped down the driveway and onto the footpath. As I skated down towards the park, I saw Frankie Halliday putting out a saucer of milk for her cat.

She spotted me and gave a shy wave, but I pretended I didn't see her. To be honest, I felt bad about the way Jasper had treated her.

Then I remembered her words. 'I'll show you,' Frankie had said. What did she mean by that?

I was still mulling it over when I reached the park. In fact, I was thinking so hard as I zoomed up the path towards the entrance that I didn't even see it coming.

BANG! I'd skated right into something and knocked myself flat on my back.

Dazed, I looked up. A two-metre high fence made of big squares of plywood loomed above me.

'Crikey,' I exclaimed. 'That wasn't there yesterday.'

I looked around. The whole park had been fenced off. The big wooden wall stretched as far as my eyes could see. There was barbed wire on top and signs saying, 'DANGEROUS! KEEP OUT!'

Boy, the Mayor hadn't wasted any time. The council workmen must have been here all night putting the fence up. The barbed wire looked scary.

If you tried to climb over the top, it would cut you to pieces.

My big problem was how to get inside. There was no way I was giving up now. If the Mayor had gone to so much trouble to keep people out, there must be a good reason.

I took my skates off and crept barefoot around the fence. I couldn't go over the top, and the only other way in was through the gate. But that was chained shut and fastened with a giant padlock. I had to think of another way. If only the others were here!

'Calm down,' I told myself. 'Think about this logically.' I tried to imagine what Toby would say in this situation.

'The workmen put this fence up in a terrible hurry,' I heard Toby's voice say quietly inside my head. *'And they did it at night, in the dark. Chances are, they've made a mistake somewhere. You just have to find it.'*

I started looking. Toby's voice was right — it was a bodgy job. Most of the boards were nailed down tightly, but some were loose. I chose one that was out of sight of the main road and started prising it open.

After ten minutes, I'd done it. My fingers were red raw, and my arms ached, but with one final yank the board came free and I was through into the park.

Victory! I propped the plank up behind me so nobody would see the hole in the fence and headed for the tree house.

Good. The ladder was still there, hidden under some bushes. It was an old extension ladder that Dad had used for his house-painting business, and didn't want any more. It was the only thing long enough to reach the tree house.

I dragged the ladder out from the bushes and propped it up against the trunk. Higher and higher I climbed, through the green leafy branches of the great fig tree, until finally, I reached the tree house.

Up this high you could see all over the district. It was like being in the crow's nest of an old wooden sailing ship.

I reached for the binoculars we kept there and trained them on our house in Tumblegum Street. No sign of Jasper — but I could see Mum and Dad sunning themselves in the backyard. Obviously they weren't worried.

Suddenly I heard voices. Someone was unlocking the padlock on the gate into the park. As it swung open, I turned the binoculars on it — and nearly fell out of the tree house with shock.

It was Mayor Fitzherbert. There was no mistaking his big red face. I also recognised the other man with him — Barry Plunder, the developer. They were carrying some big sheets of paper and they were heading straight for the fig tree.

'This is where the 20-storey high-rise tower will go,' I heard Barry Plunder say, 'overlooking all the other apartment blocks. We'll have to cut this tree down, of course.'

I held my breath. They were right underneath me. Now I could see what the sheets of paper were. They were building plans.

'Very nice,' said the Mayor. 'The penthouse will get a lovely breeze up on this ridge. The sort of place I'd like to retire to, in fact!'

Mr Plunder chuckled. 'I'm sure we can make some arrangement, Mayor,' he said in his slimy voice. 'As soon as council approves the plan, that is . . .'

The Mayor nodded eagerly, his jowls wobbling. 'This Tuesday, Barry. I've organised a late-night council meeting. We can rush it through when all the councillors are half-asleep. And of course, there shouldn't be anyone in the public gallery at that time.'

Barry Plunder nodded. 'Well, there's no need for the residents to know just yet. Why worry them when it's all in their best interests?'

I could hardly believe what I was hearing. No wonder the Mayor wanted to close the park. He and

Barry Plunder were plotting to turn it into a giant high-rise tower!

'What was that?' The Mayor looked around nervously.

I'd heard the noise too. Click. Click. It sounded familiar but I couldn't put my finger on it. It was coming from the bushes where we hid the ladder. I turned around to get a better look, and as I did, I dropped the binoculars.

CRASH!

Startled, the two men looked up — straight into my hiding place.

I heard a rustle from the bushes, but the two men didn't seem to notice. Their eyes were fixed on mine and they looked mean and angry. The Mayor's face turned so red I thought his head was going to explode.

There was nothing I could do. There was nowhere to run. I was trapped.

Chapter Six

Meanwhile, Jasper was right in the middle of her own adventure.

It all started when we split up at the Cave. While I headed home to pick up some provisions, Jasper stayed back to get her instructions from Toby.

'Right-o, you'd better get cracking,' he told her. 'I want three photo-stories from you by the end of the day. First, the three-legged dog. Second, see if the twins have started their hunger strike yet, and get a picture if they have. Any time you've got left, you can start work on the Stackett investigation.'

Toby was taking his job as editor seriously but as you can imagine, Jasper had to put her two cents worth in. 'Why can't I do the Stackett's first?' she argued. 'That's the most interesting story.'

'It's also the most dangerous,' Toby pointed out. 'If you're discovered sneaking around their house there's no telling what might happen. This way, we'll at least have two stories in the can if you get caught.'

'I guess that makes sense,' agreed Jasper. 'What are you going to do?'

'I'll stay here and start laying out the front page. Now that we know what stories we'll be doing, I can decide where to put them. It's a bit like putting a jigsaw puzzle together.'

'A jigsaw puzzle! I'm glad you're doing it, I'm terrible at them. See you later.'

'Good luck. And make sure you check in with me before you go to the Stackett's. Just to be safe,' Toby said.

The three-legged dog story didn't take long. The Fletchers were so pleased to be starring in our newspaper that they even let Jasper put a baseball cap and sunglasses on the puppy while he had his photo taken.

After that, she called by the twins' house, but nobody was home. Checking that her camera was wound on and ready to take another picture, Jasper set off towards the Stackett's ahead of schedule. She'd already decided to cut through the Trotter's backyard — that way, she could approach the house without being seen from the road and check in with Toby.

The door to the Cave was shut, so Jasper decided not to bother Toby. There'd be plenty of time later to tell him about the dog. If all went according to plan, she'd be in and out of the Stackett's house within half an hour — hopefully with the photographs she wanted.

Jasper crept through the hole in the fence and crouched in the bushes on the other side. There was no sign of movement from the Stackett's house, but she could hear a washing machine churning in the outside laundry. Good. That was an important clue.

'Mrs Stackett must be inside, but she'll have to come out at some point to hang the washing on the line,' Jasper thought out loud, pleased with her detective work. 'That's my chance to get inside the house and find the prisoner.'

The problem was, where could she hide while she was waiting? If she stayed where she was, Mrs Stackett would probably see her as she dashed across to the back door. It was too big a risk to take. She had to get closer to the house.

Jasper peered through the leaves of the bush. The only possible hiding place was underneath the back stairs. There were only three of them. Jasper squinted, trying to see if she could fit into the small space underneath.

'I'll have to take the chance,' she thought. 'The washing machine could stop any moment now.'

Her heart pounding, Jasper ran like lightning across the backyard. She made it just in time. As she squeezed herself into the tiny space underneath the stairs, the washing machine gave a final thump and whirred into silence.

Jasper heard a slow, clumping noise. Then, the back door opened. The clumping changed to a shuffle as old Mrs Stackett eased herself towards the top step.

Jasper peered through the space in the stairs, just in time to look straight up old Mrs Stackett's skirt.

After what seemed like a century, old Mrs Stackett reached the bottom of the stairs. Jasper watched as she limped slowly into the laundry.

The coast was clear. It was now or never.

Five seconds later, Jasper was inside the Stackett's house.

Of course, I had no idea any of that was happening until later. I had my own problems to worry about.

The Mayor was furious. Peering down at him from the tree house, I could hear him huffing and puffing. He looked like a big balloon, just about to burst.

'YOU ... YOU ... troublemaker!' he shouted. Looking down at his red balloon face, I felt safe enough to give him a small, cheerful wave. After all, there was no way he could climb up the ladder to get me — he was too fat.

Barry Plunder looked mad too. 'What are we going to do?' he demanded, jabbing the Mayor in the chest. 'The boy's heard everything.'

'That's right, Mayor,' I said. 'And I've written it all down.' I waved my notebook at him. 'Come and get it if you like. Otherwise you'll have to read about it in our newspaper.'

'Go on, Barry,' ordered the Mayor. 'Climb up the ladder and grab that little troublemaker's notebook.'

Mr Plunder went pale.

'I can't, Cecil. I'm scared of heights.'

'Well, I've got a heart condition,' snapped the Mayor. They stared at each other crossly.

'Come on up,' I prompted. 'I'll race you to the top of the tree.'

Barry Plunder went from white to green, and groaned. The Mayor glared at me.

'You little smart alec. Just wait till I get my hands on you . . .'

His eyes suddenly lit up. Scanning the ground, he picked up a rock the size of an egg.

'This'll fix you!' he shouted. 'I'll flush you out!'

The Mayor lobbed the rock up at me like it was a hand grenade. Unfortunately for him, it hit a branch on the way up, and bounced back and hit him on the head.

'YOW! OW! OW! OW!' The Mayor danced around, clutching his head and howling like a dog.

'I think you need some target practice, Mayor,' I called out.

The Mayor rubbed his head, stumped. Then, a wily expression crossed his face. 'Come on, boy. Let's be friends, hey? You're a smart kid,' he said. A slimy smile spread over his fat face. 'You know I wouldn't do something unless it was a good thing for Blue Rock.'

Looking down at him, I wasn't so sure. I had a feeling he was trying to sweet-talk me.

'Tell you what,' said the Mayor, rubbing his hands together. 'I'll make a deal with you. Let's call it a business deal.'

I didn't say anything. What was he up to?

'Give me the notebook, boy,' continued the Mayor in a soft, friendly tone. 'And I'll buy you a special present. What'll it be — the latest computer game? A new bike?'

I sat in the tree house and stared out over Blue Rock. The only sound was the wind through the leaves, and a passing car.

'I'll give you anything you want,' wheedled the Mayor. 'And we'll forget this ever happened.'

I thought about what he said as I looked out from the tree house. My eye travelled the length of Tumblegum Street and came to rest on the old tin roof of the Cave. I remembered the Friendship Tower we had made that morning, and the words of the oath rang in my ears.

'*I swear to seek the truth and when I find it, to tell it without fear or favour.*'

Without fear or favour. Suddenly, I understood what it meant. The Mayor had tried to frighten me into not writing the story. That was the fear. Then he'd tried to bribe me. That was the favour.

I knew exactly what I had to do.

'No deal, Mayor,' I said. 'The people of Blue Rock deserve to know the truth about what you're doing with our park. And I'm going to tell them.'

The Mayor shook his fist at me. He didn't look friendly any more. 'You stupid boy!' he shouted. 'You'll regret this!'

He turned to Barry Plunder. 'Quick, help me move the ladder. A couple of nights out here on his own might change the little troublemaker's mind.'

'Hey!' I yelled. 'You can't do that! Nobody knows I'm here! I'll starve to death!'

Barry Plunder chuckled. 'It'll do you good to go

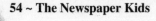

hungry. Anyway, it's only until Wednesday morning. As soon as our plans are approved, we'll make sure somebody finds you.'

I watched helplessly as the two men lowered the ladder onto the ground.

'You'll go to jail for this,' I said desperately. 'You can't leave me here for nights on my own. I'll tell everyone when I get down, anyway.'

The Mayor shrugged. 'Who's going to believe you?' he said as the two of them walked away. 'You're only a kid.'

I sat down on the floor of the tree house and put my head in my hands.

What a terrible jam I was in. I was trapped in a tree house — and for the first time in my life, I found myself missing Jasper.

But Jasper wasn't missing me. In fact, she hadn't even thought about me.

Chapter Seven

At that exact moment, Jasper was creeping down the hallway of the Stackett's house.

Hearing about it later made me break out in goosebumps.

'It was like being in a haunted house,' she told us in hushed tones. 'Even though the sun was shining outside, it was all dark and quiet. It reminded me of being in a tomb in a graveyard and the whole place stank of mothballs. I nearly choked. Every room I passed I expected to see old Mr Stackett sitting there — propped up in a pile of mothballs so he wouldn't rot. I just held my nose and hoped Mrs Stackett had left an arm or a leg poking out so I'd see him.'

But except for a few bits of old furniture, and piles of junk, the rooms were empty. Heavy blinds and curtains shut out almost every bit of light.

Jasper's fear turned to frustration. Where was old Mr Stackett? All she needed was a quick photograph and she could escape by the front door.

There was only one room left to check.

Jasper crept towards the doorway. Like the other rooms, it seemed to be in darkness. But there was one difference. This room had voices coming from it.

'Oh, Ridge, Ridge!' Jasper heard a woman's voice saying. 'Marry me! Let's run away together and be happy!'

'I can't, Alexis,' a man's deep voice replied. 'I'm already married, and so are you. Besides, you probably don't realise this, but I am actually your long-lost twin brother who was kidnapped at birth and later adopted by your arch-enemy, Victoria.'

Jasper's eyes popped. What a story! She peeked around the doorway, then realised what she was hearing.

It was a television. And somebody was watching it. Somebody sitting in a chair with their back to my sister.

Jasper's heart was pounding so loudly she was certain it could be heard above the television.

But the person sitting in the chair didn't move.

Maybe we were right, thought Jasper. Maybe old Mr Stackett is dead, and Mrs Stackett just keeps his body here and talks to it.

Jasper shivered. With shaking hands, she checked that the flash on her camera was switched on. For the hundredth time, she checked the film was wound on. It was time. There was no going back.

With slow, silent steps, she walked towards the chair. Her heartbeat was like a cannonball thumping against her chest but Jasper was so scared she hardly heard it.

Anyone else — including me — would have turned and run right out of there. But not Jasper. Something gave her the courage to walk up to that chair and look at the person sitting there. And what she saw made her whole body go cold and numb.

Staring back at her was the face of a monster.

It was an old, old man. But his face wasn't completely human — one side of it was twisted into a terrible mask. One eye squinted fiercely; the other was wide open and staring. The mouth was a leering grimace. And as cold fingers of fear paralysed my sister's body, she heard a low, strangled moan.

The monster was trying to speak.

Jasper screamed, and fell to the floor in a dead faint.

By five o'clock that afternoon, Toby was starting to

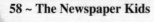

get worried. He hadn't seen either of us all day and it was getting dark. His frantic messages to our computer went unanswered. Obviously, we weren't at home.

Toby was faced with a dilemma. He knew our parents would have a double-barrelled heart attack if they knew Jasper and I were out alone after dark and might even put a stop to our newspaper, but on the other hand, what if we were in trouble?

He looked at his watch. Twenty-past five. Time was running out. In no time at all, it would be pitch black.

With a heavy heart, he made his decision.

'Toby!' It was Dad who answered the door. He looked annoyed. 'We were just about to come looking. Where are those two rascals?'

Toby gulped. 'I don't know, Mr Lilley.'

'Well, I want an answer. I've just had Mr and Mrs Quinn down here, complaining that their girls won't eat anything. Not only that, they've been waving some sort of protest banners outside their house. Very embarrassing. The twins say that you three put them up to it.'

'Oh.' Toby blushed. 'The hunger strike.'

'A *hunger* strike?' Dad fumed. 'I've never heard anything so ridiculous in my life! Those two are going to cop it and as for you, young man, I'm very disappointed. I thought you had more sense than that!'

Toby hung his head.

'Come on, son — you can't protect Hugo and Jasper forever. Where are they hiding?'

'I don't know. Honestly, Mr Lilley. I haven't seen them all day.'

Dad looked alarmed. 'What do you mean? We thought they were with you.'

Toby knew that in approximately seven seconds, all hell was going to break loose. But there was no way out. He had to tell them.

'Hugo and Jasper are missing,' he said. 'I think we should send out a search party.'

Up in the tree house, it was getting chilly. I stuck my head out of the doorway and peered down, hoping that something might have changed since the last time I looked.

No such luck. If anything, the ground was further away than ever. Once again, I found myself wishing we'd built the tree house closer to the ground. Why, oh why, had I insisted it be this high? Without a ladder there was just no way of getting down.

I had already contemplated trying to climb down through the branches, but just the thought of it made my stomach curl into a tight ball. The tree house was perched way out on a branch. I'd fall for sure. And the only thing I could possibly make a rope from — a

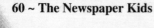

silly gingham tablecloth Jasper had insisted on bringing here — was too short. I'd need at least twenty of them tied together. One was no use at all.

As the light faded, I debated whether to light a candle. We only had three, and two of them were already halfway burnt down. I'd be lucky if they lasted a night. And I could be stuck here until Wednesday!

Well, at least I had some food in my day-pack. If I rationed it, it would probably last for two, possibly three days. I started to unwrap a muesli bar, then thought better of it. Better to save it until I was really hungry.

The cold was starting to worry me. It was almost winter, and at home, we'd already started using our electric blankets. Gloomily, I wondered how cold it had to be before someone froze to death. I remembered stories about explorers who had survived for weeks in the snow. They said fifty percent of body heat escaped through your head.

I grabbed the gingham tablecloth and wrapped it around my head like a turban. Maybe it wasn't so useless after all. I didn't care how stupid I looked. I just had to keep warm.

As the dying rays of the sun slipped below the horizon. I got up for a last look out of the tree house.

Tears sprang to my eyes as I looked down on

Tumblegum Street and found my house. My home. My heart ached as I thought of my bedroom — the familiar old green bedspread, and the glow-in-the-dark planets and stars stuck on the ceiling.

Suddenly, I saw some movement in Tumblegum Street. I strained my eyes to see in the fading light. There were people running from house to house — three or four of them.

I couldn't make out who they were, but they seemed to be in a bit of a panic, criss-crossing the road, almost banging into each other, as they rushed from one house to the next. From where I was, they looked like frantic ants.

'What are they doing?' I thought, puzzled. 'Are they looking for something?' Then it struck me. 'Maybe they're looking for me!'

Of course! Mum and Dad would be worried sick that I hadn't come home.

Then my heart sank. They'd never come here. The park was fenced off with barbed wire. Besides, it was out of bounds to Jasper and me. Unless somebody stumbled on my loose plank by pure fluke, I'd be stuck here for days, right under their noses.

I had to get their attention somehow. Fumbling in the dark, I found the torch. We'd never had any reason to use it. I didn't even know if it had batteries in it.

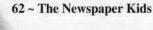

I switched it on, and breathed a sigh of relief. A weak light shone out. It wasn't much — but it might be enough.

I stood at the window of the tree house and prayed that someone in the search party would see what I was about to do. Shining the torch out into the darkness, I started to switch it on and off. Three short flashes. Three long flashes. Then three short flashes again.

SOS. That's what it meant in morse code. The international signal meaning someone in distress.

SOS. SOS.

The torch lasted long enough for me to send three distress signals. Then the light sputtered and died.

I was in darkness again. I strained my ears, but the only sound was the wind whistling eerily through the leaves of the old fig tree.

It hadn't worked. No one had seen my signal. I crouched in the corner of the tree house with my head in my hands. My only hope of being discovered had been crushed. I was on my own.

I don't know how long I sat there like that before I heard them. It felt like hours but it was probably only about three minutes.

I could hear running footsteps on the road outside the park. Voices. Somebody rattling the gate and yelling.

And then the best sound I'd ever heard in my life. Cutting through the black night, I heard my dad's voice, shouting my name as clear as day.

'Hugo! Hugo, are you in there?'

Chapter Eight

'**D**on't say a word.' Dad's face was grim as he marched me up Tumblegum Street towards home. Toby and Mr Trotter followed in silence.

'Ouch!' I yelped. 'I'd really like to keep that arm in its socket, Dad. Listen. It wasn't my fault, it was . . .'

'Quiet!' thundered Dad. I'd never seen him so angry. 'Save your breath until we see your mother. She's still looking for Jasper. The pair of you had better have a good explanation.'

I gulped. By the sound of it, it was going to be a major inquisition. Mr Trotter caught my eye and winked at me. Well, that was something. At least *he* was on my side. Maybe I could go and live with the Trotters when Dad kicked me out of home. Maybe Mr Trotter could adopt me. But what if he didn't take Jasper as well? I'd have to sneak food scraps out to her . . .

A loud shriek interrupted my train of thought.

'Let me go! Aaaggh! You're killing me!' No mistaking the voice — it was Jasper.

I looked up.

Mum was dragging old Bossy Boots down the front steps of the Stacketts' house by the ear, and Jasper was screaming blue murder.

The Stacketts' house! She'd been inside!

'This is child abuse!' yelled Jasper. 'I'll have to report you to the authorities, Mother. In fact, I'll DIVORCE you! Kids can divorce their parents, you know. They do in America.'

Mum looked frazzled. She saw Dad, then she saw me, and her face lit up with relief.

'Nick! Where did you find him?'

'Up a tree, of all places. In the park.' He glared at me. 'Toby saw him flashing a torch, or he'd still be there.'

'Well, I found Madam sitting in the Stacketts' kitchen like the Queen of Sheba, eating scones and jam, if you please.'

'They invited me,' said Jasper sulkily, rubbing

her ear. 'I had lunch there, too. They *liked* me being there.'

Mum turned on her. 'You shouldn't have bothered them! Poor old Mrs Stackett has enough on her plate, now that her husband . . .'

She broke off, and marched ahead in silence. I was itching with curiosity. What *was* it about old Mr Stackett? Why did we have to stay away?

When we reached the front gate, Dad shook Mr Trotter's hand.

'Thanks for your help, David,' he said. 'I'm sure you'll understand if we keep the kids away from your place for a couple of weeks. Not that I think Toby's a bad influence on them.' He looked darkly at Jasper and me. 'Quite the opposite in fact.'

The three of us listened helplessly. Banned from seeing each other! How could we get our newspaper out in time to save the park? I knew from what the Mayor said that the council would approve Barry Plunder's plans on Tuesday night. It was Sunday night now. That gave us just over one day to let the people of Blue Rock know what was going on.

One day. That wasn't just a tough deadline. It was impossible.

'But Dad . . .' I started.

'Dad, that's not fair . . .'

Dad cut us off without even listening.

'Inside, you two,' he snapped. 'I want an explanation. And it better be good.'

Grounded! We couldn't believe it.

'The two of you are confined to this house for the next two weeks,' Mum ordered. 'You are not to step outside unless you are supervised by one of us.'

'And don't even think about playing with Toby in that period of time,' added Dad sternly.

The way they were acting, you'd think we'd committed the worst crime in history.

'You mean he can't even visit us?' wailed Jasper. 'But that's illegal. We have rights, you know . . .'

'Fine. When we move to America you can divorce us,' said Mum impatiently. 'Until then, you're grounded. Without visitors. And you are not to use the phone.'

'But what about our newspaper?' I was desperate. We were onto a huge story — and now it looked like nobody would ever get to read it.

'That newspaper!' Dad exploded. 'If it wasn't for that newspaper, you wouldn't be in this trouble. Poking your noses in where they're not supposed to be. Organising protests. Pestering the neighbours. And worrying your mother and me half to death!'

I gave it one last try.

'The Mayor's going to put a high-rise tower up in our park and we're the only ones that can stop him,' I said stubbornly. 'That's why he left me trapped in the tree. Don't you understand?'

'Oh, Hugo.' Mum shook her head. 'You could make movies with that imagination of yours. The Mayor's got far more important things to do than chase kids up trees.'

'Anyway,' added Dad, 'you can't just accuse people of things like that without proof. It's called libel. There are laws against it.'

There was no point arguing. They'd made up their minds. Our grand plans to save the park had been smashed. Our newspaper had been banned before it even hit the streets. And now, we couldn't even talk to each other.

'What a disaster!' I stormed through the door that connected my room to Jasper's and flung myself onto her bed. 'Hey! What are you doing?'

'What does it look like I'm doing? Tap dancing?'

'It looks like you're sending a message to Toby,' I said uneasily.

Jasper was standing at the computer tapping into it.

'My brother the rocket scientist,' muttered Jasper. 'Give yourself a gold star, Hugo.'

'But we're not allowed to.' I jumped up and grabbed her arm. 'Mum and Dad will kill us!'

'We're not allowed to use the *phone*, Hugo. They never said anything about the computer. Or the modem.'

I shrugged and let her go. That was the good thing about our parents — they tended to forget about the existence of computers. I wondered what people over thirty had used when they were at school. Stone tablets?

Jasper frowned.

'That's funny,' she said. 'I can't get through to Myron. He won't take the message.'

I looked over her shoulder. The computer screen said simply, 'No access. User error.'

'It's never done that before,' I said. 'Try again.'

'I've tried heaps of times already.' Jasper turned to me. 'Something's wrong.'

'Maybe Toby's turned Myron off for the night. He does that sometimes.'

Jasper shook her head. 'It shouldn't make any difference. The computer simply stores the message. Besides, Toby would be waiting to hear from us. It's the only way we've got to communicate.'

She was right. In fact, it was odd that Toby hadn't already contacted us.

Jasper opened the door of the bedroom and

listened carefully. Downstairs, we could hear the television blaring. Mum and Dad were watching the Sunday night movie.

'Come on,' she whispered. 'We've got at least half an hour before they check on us again.'

The next thing I knew she'd opened the window next to her bed and started climbing out.

'You're nuts,' I said desperately. 'We're already grounded for two weeks. Do you want us to be locked up for life?'

I could hear the ivy-covered trellis shaking as Jasper's head disappeared from view.

'Stop worrying,' I heard her say. 'We'll get ourselves a good lawyer.'

My runners hit the ground with a thud as I jumped the last two metres from the trellis.

'Shut up!' Jasper whispered fiercely. 'You sound like a herd of elephants.'

She turned and disappeared into the darkness.

'Hey, Jasper,' I panted as we cut across the Stacketts' backyard towards Toby's. 'You never told me what happened to you. Did you get the photo of old Mr Stackett?'

'Of course I got the photo.' Jasper squeezed through the fence into Toby's yard. I followed as fast as I could, puffing.

'Well?'

'Well what?' Jasper asked.

I couldn't see Jasper's face, but the back of her head looked mighty smug.

'Well, what does he look like?'

'Forget what he looks like, Hugo. The photo's not important. It's the story that matters.'

'So tell me the story!' How frustrating can a sister be?

'Not now,' said Jasper crisply. 'You'll just have to wait until I've written it.'

'I thought you said you wanted to be a photographer.'

'I do. But there's no reason I can't write as well. I guess I'm just an all-round genius.'

Jasper was lucky we'd reached the Cave by then, or I would have thumped her.

The light was on, and the door was ajar. As we pushed it open, I could see Toby sitting in front of Myron.

As soon as he turned around I knew something was wrong. Toby didn't even look surprised to see us. In fact, there was no expression at all on his face. He looked like he was in shock.

'I thought you'd come,' he said dully. 'I've been waiting.'

'We've been trying to contact you,' said Jasper

breathlessly. 'But we couldn't get through, the computer . . .'

Toby stood up from his chair and gestured at Myron. At first glance, it looked like the whole screen was alive with words. But up close, you could see they weren't words at all. They were symbols — computer symbols, the sort that programs were written in. There were millions of them, scrolling upwards so fast they became one indecipherable blur.

Myron had gone haywire.

'It's been like that ever since I got back from your place.' Toby's voice was calm, but his face was white and I could see his hands shaking.

Jasper and I stared at the screen, speechless. I felt sick. Somewhere in that jumble of computer jibberish was our newspaper.

'It's a virus.' Toby tapped randomly at the keyboard. 'See what happens when I touch any of the keys?'

Huge black letters rolled across the screen.

HA! HA! HA! HA! HA! HA!

'Turn it off! Make it stop!' cried Jasper hysterically. 'It's laughing at us!'

I still couldn't believe it. 'How could it happen?' I asked Toby. 'Myron's got an anti-virus program hasn't he?'

'Of course. But it only picks up the common

viruses.' He frowned. 'I've never seen this one before. It's extremely destructive. From what I can tell, we've lost the lot. The stories, the headlines, the whole program.'

'But I don't understand!' I was getting angry. 'Nobody except us has used this computer. Ever. The Cave is locked up whenever we're not here. How could anybody get to it?'

Toby didn't say a word. He simply pointed to the desk. I looked over, and groaned. Of course. The computer disks. There were dozens of them. Every one of them had been written on and delivered by an outside person. Any one of them could have been contaminated.

'The person who sabotaged the computer didn't even have to break in,' said Toby. 'Don't you see? We virtually gave them an invitation.'

I was in bed no more than thirty seconds when Dad put his head in the door to say good night.

'By the way, one of your friends was looking for you earlier,' he said. 'The Halliday girl — Frankie, isn't it? David Trotter found her poking around that old shed you kids use. Said she had something important to tell you.'

'Yeah? Did she say what?' This was major information so I tried to sound casual.

'No idea. But whatever it is, it'll have to wait. Don't forget, digger — two weeks and not a day less.'

I mumbled good night, pretending to be sleepy, but my mind was buzzing.

Frankie Halliday. *Poking around that old shed.*

'I'll show you,' she had said.

Was Frankie Halliday the one who sabotaged the newspaper? The question was still clanging in my brain as I finally fell asleep.

Chapter Nine

'I should have guessed,' fumed Jasper. 'Just wait until I get my hands on her . . .'

'Well, hang on a minute.' I was starting to regret passing on my hunch. 'We can't say for sure that Frankie did it. We don't have any proof.'

'Of course she did it!' Jasper flared. 'She's ruined our newspaper, just like she said she would. Who else would it be?'

'It could be the Mayor,' I said. 'He stands to lose more than anyone else if we publish my story. He might even go to jail.'

Toby, hot off the trellis, was standing with us in Jasper's room, brushing twigs and leaves off his jumper.

'Except Barry Plunder,' he said. 'Don't forget him. He'll make a lot of money if this development goes through. Maybe millions. He could easily get his hands on a virus, too. He's got a whole team of computer experts working for him and . . .'

'Jasper! Hugo!' The three of us froze as we heard the clickety-click of high heels moving along the hallway outside.

'Quick! It's Mum! Get in the bathroom!' I grabbed Toby and shoved him into the shower recess just as Mum opened the door.

'I'm going to visit Great-aunt Miranda,' she said, smiling at Jasper and me. 'I know you'll do the right thing if I leave you here alone. You'll stick to the agreement we made? Word of honour?'

She looked so trusting, and it seemed so terrible to deceive her, that I almost opened my mouth and blabbed everything. A sharp pinch from Jasper brought me back to earth.

'Of course we will, Mum,' she said innocently. 'Word of honour.'

'You're shameless,' I groaned after Mum had gone. Toby emerged from the shower, wiping his wet shoes on the bathmat.

'I'm not,' protested Jasper. 'We promised we wouldn't play with Toby, and we're not. This is business.'

'They said no visitors.' I still wasn't convinced.

'He's not a visitor because this isn't a social occasion,' argued Jasper. 'It's work, and he's a business partner. It all depends how you look at it.'

'I hate to remind you,' interrupted Toby, 'but we've got one day to get a newspaper out and we're starting from scratch. Let's debate the details later.'

Good old Toby. He was always so practical. When the virus crashed his computer and destroyed all our newspaper work with it, we thought that was the end of it. But we hadn't counted on Toby making copies. And neither, I guess, had the person who tried to sabotage us with a virus-infected floppy disk. Luckily, before he went to bed, Toby had printed out the day's work and kept it in a special folder in his bedroom. So we still had all our 'Community Billboard' stories, as well as the social pages, Dr Death, the sports reports, our jokes and riddles section, and Toby's first editorial, which explained what the paper was all about.

'Your computer uses pretty much the same desktop publishing program as Myron, so it's just a matter of entering the information again.' Toby clicked the mouse quickly as he checked out the various functions. 'It's not quite as fancy, but it'll do the job.'

We decided that because my story was the front page lead, I would go downstairs and write it on Dad's computer, then transfer it by disk onto ours. Jasper's task was more complicated. She had to write her stories on paper, then give them to Toby to type in while she ran down to the shopping centre to get her film developed. With Myron down, it was going to be a race against time and I, for one, had my doubts we'd make it.

One other thing was worrying me. 'Dad said we need proof about the Mayor's involvement,' I told Toby. 'Otherwise, if we write something bad about him and it's wrong, we're the ones who could end up in jail.'

Toby frowned. 'I know. You're absolutely sure of your facts, Hugo?'

I took a deep breath and nodded.

'Then the decision is up to me, as editor. And I say we go with it. If the worst comes to the worst, I can always argue that it's in the public interest.'

Sitting down to start my story, I realised I was glad I wasn't the editor. Being just a plain old chief reporter somehow seemed a lot easier.

Rat-tat-tat!

I heard the knock at the front door, and ran into Jasper in the hallway as we both went to answer it.

'It's that skunk Frankie Halliday,' she hissed. 'I looked out the window. I can't believe she has the guts to show her face.'

She threw open the front door. 'Come to gloat, have you?'

Frankie looked startled. 'No . . . actually, I came to see Hugo.'

'You came to see Hugo?' mimicked Jasper nastily. 'You've got a cheek! Trying to wreck our newspaper, then showing up here like little Miss Innocent.'

Frankie shook her head. 'I don't know what you're talking about, Jasper. Honestly.' She looked at me and held up a brown paper bag she was carrying. 'I thought Hugo might need these for your story about the park.'

'I think you'd better leave,' said Jasper coldly. 'We already told you we don't want your help. Anyway, we know it was you who . . .'

'Shut up for two seconds, Jasper.' I pushed her aside.

Frankie looked at me gratefully and handed me the bag.

'Hugo!' Jasper was furious. 'It's probably another disk with a virus on it. I can't believe you're trusting her. If you don't close this door RIGHT NOW . . .'

I opened the bag. As I pulled out the contents, Jasper's voice dried up mid-sentence.

They were photos, black and white ones, of the Mayor and Barry Plunder standing together, looking at something. Then a closer shot. Looking at a building plan. Then another close-up. So close you could see a thumbnail with a jagged edge where someone had chewed it. The thumb was part of a hand that was holding onto the building plan. A plan that showed huge high-rise buildings all over the land that used to be our park . . .

'Where did you get these?' I was so shocked my voice was no louder than a whisper.

'In the park,' said Frankie. 'I followed you in . . .'

I interrupted. 'Why didn't I see you?'

'I was hiding in the bushes. I had my telephoto lens on the camera. It means I can take close-ups from a long way away. It's like looking through a telescope.'

The bushes! Of course! That was the noise I heard. It was the clicking of Frankie's camera.

'As soon as they saw you in the tree house I took off,' Frankie continued. 'I knew you'd want the photos so I went straight to my darkroom and developed them.'

'So you didn't realise they took the ladder away? Left me trapped in the tree house?'

Frankie's eyes widened. 'No! How did you . . .'

'Never mind.' I grabbed Frankie's arm and pulled her inside.

'Hmmph!' Jasper looked miffed but she didn't try to stop me. 'Mum said no visitors . . .'

'Frankie's not a visitor,' I said, throwing my arm around Frankie's shoulders. We looked at each other and grinned. 'She's a business partner.'

'Hey! This Stackett story's not bad, sis!'

Jasper tried to look modest, then gave up. 'I know. I'm pretty pleased with it myself. What do you think of the headline Toby put on it?'

'OUR NEIGHBOURS NEED OUR HELP,' it said in bold type with 'by Jasper Lilley' underneath.

'That's the part I like,' said Jasper proudly. 'My name in print!'

I read the story out loud:

> The other day I went to visit our next-door neighbours, the Stacketts. They are both very old — Mrs Stackett is eighty-two and Mr Stackett is eighty-three. The sad thing is that nobody ever goes to visit them because their children have all grown up and moved away, and most of their friends have died. My brother and I used to be scared of them, but now I know they are lonely and like to have company. Mrs Stackett has a bad leg and can't get around very easily and Mr Stackett is very sick.

He had a stroke twelve months ago. That means he is in a wheelchair and, as you can see by the photo, one side of his body doesn't work at all.

'Ed would really love to go outside in the sunshine but I can't manage to get him down the stairs in the wheelchair,' Mrs Stackett told me. 'It's hard enough just doing the cooking and cleaning, what with my bad leg.'

The Stacketts don't want to leave their house but, if nobody helps them, they will have to go into a old people's home. I hope that doesn't happen because they have lots of interesting stories to tell. Mr Stackett is really funny, too, you just have to listen to him carefully because he can't speak quickly. I am going to ask my dad to get Mr Stackett's wheelchair down the stairs so he can go outside, and maybe you can do the same. It would make a big difference to the Stacketts' lives!

'So that's why we never saw him!' I exclaimed. Suddenly the whole thing made sense. 'It must be terrible being stuck inside with nobody else to talk to.'

'It is. Mrs Stackett says she's heard all of Mr Stackett's jokes so many times that she doesn't even laugh at them anymore.'

Toby looked up from the computer. 'We're lucky that Frankie is going to print the photographs for us in her darkroom. She was right, you know. There's no way we'd get them done in time otherwise.'

Frankie blushed. 'It's no trouble, really. I'm happy to help.'

'What headline have you put on Hugo's story, Toby?' asked Jasper hastily, changing the subject. She was embarrassed she'd treated Frankie so badly and I knew she'd take a bit of time to get over it.

'I thought I'd keep it simple,' said Toby. 'Here. Take a look at the dummy run.' He pulled out a sheet of paper.

'SAVE OUR PARK,' it said in giant letters. And underneath, 'by Chief Reporter Hugo Lilley. Photographs by Frankie Halliday.'

'That'll be right across the top of the front page,' said Toby. 'I just have to work out where to put the photographs. Then I thought I'd run the editorial down one side, telling people what the paper's all about.'

'You could call it "Welcome to . . ." whatever we call the paper,' suggested Jasper. 'Come to think of it, Toby, what *are* we going to call it?'

'Yeah, we don't have a lot of time left,' I said. 'That's an idea . . . how about the *Tumblegum Times*?'

Toby shook his head. 'Too boring. It sounds like a grown-up's paper.'

We sat in silence, thinking hard.

Jasper jumped up. 'I know! How about the *Blue Rock Crier*? Telling people what's going on, as in town crier?'

'As in cry-baby,' I said scornfully. 'That's a dumb name.'

'All right then, how about the *Big Blabbermouth*, after you?' retorted Jasper angrily. 'You always tell everyone what's going on, even when you're not supposed to.'

'Oh, settle down,' sighed Toby. He drummed his fingers impatiently on the desk. 'How about *Street Sheet*? As in, a sheet of paper about our street?'

Mmmmm . . . that was close. But it sounded too much like bed-linen. Street something . . . street . . . street . . .

'How about *Street Wise*?' It was Frankie who finally broke the silence. 'That's what you call someone who's tough and cool and knows what's happening out on the streets. That's sort of what the paper is like, isn't it?'

We looked at Frankie, then we looked at each other.

'She's right, you know.'

I could hardly believe my ears. It was Jasper. She still wasn't looking Frankie in the eye, but there was something in her voice I hadn't heard before — a grudging respect.

'It's a brilliant name,' she continued. She looked at Frankie and smiled. 'Let's call the paper *Street Wise*.'

So we did.

Luckily Mum and Dad thought we were asleep and didn't bother us as we worked until half-past eleven that night — writing articles, putting headlines on them, scanning in photographs, printing out pages and finally, stapling them together to make our six-page newspaper, *Street Wise*.

'There, that's the last of them,' announced Toby, red-eyed with exhaustion. 'Let's get some sleep before we drop dead.'

We all knew that we needed our strength for the next day. By eight am, *Street Wise* had to be on the streets. Toby and Frankie would be selling it at bus stops, at the shopping centre, and door to door.

'What if nobody buys it?' I asked. 'What if we got it all wrong?'

Toby blinked at us wearily through his thick glasses. 'We've done our best,' he said. 'What happens now is anyone's guess.'

Chapter Ten

'If I eat another thing, I am going to explode.' Jasper flopped down onto the grass, groaning.

'Then let me jump on your stomach,' I offered. 'That could be my good deed for the day.'

'Don't you dare.' She flicked me lazily with one of her long orange plaits as we lay sprawled in the shade, the smell of the sausage sizzle wafting over us. 'Can you believe how many people are here?'

I looked around. It was a warm, sunny day, and people had been pouring through the gates since ten o'clock. There were hundreds of them. In fact, it was the first time I'd seen almost every person in Blue

Rock together in the one place. Even Ms Finch, the grade five teacher, had dragged herself out of bed early to lend a hand. She was on the face-painting stall, which was just as well because she'd had heaps of practice on her own face. By the time Jasper and I got there, we hardly recognised the place. There was even a bush band playing — and you could tell by the way people's feet were jigging around that pretty soon they'd be up dancing. The park didn't look like a park any more — it looked like a giant carnival.

'Just think, if it wasn't for us, this wouldn't be happening,' I said.

'I know. They'd be ripping it apart with bulldozers instead.' Jasper sat up and waved at somebody in the crowd. 'Look! Here come the Stacketts.'

'Yoo-hoo! Howdy-hoo!' Old Mr Stackett zoomed towards us on his new electric wheelchair, cackling like a maniac. The crowd scattered to get out of his way. Old Mrs Stackett followed him slowly on foot, tut-tutting.

'How do you like this, kids? Four-wheel drive wheelchair! I can go up and down sand dunes on this thing!' Even though he was excited, Mr Stackett spoke slowly. Although now that Mr Stackett was getting out of the house so much, he hardly ever stopped talking.

He screeched to a halt in his wheelchair, then

pressed his finger hard on one of the buttons and did a 360 degree turn. 'Whooo-eee! Hey, did you hear the one about the camel that thought it was a . . .'

'Edgar!' Old Mrs Stackett finally caught up, puffing. 'Everyone's heard all of your jokes at least a hundred times. Now take it easy on that thing or you'll . . .'

'Stack it!' yelled old Mr Stackett. 'Heh, heh! Get it, Maisie? I'll stack it!'

'Silly old fool,' grumbled old Mrs Stackett, but she had a twinkle in her eye. In fact, I'd never seen her so happy. And it was all thanks to Jasper's story.

You see, once people realised what was wrong, they all wanted to help. Two days after *Street Wise* came out, the Stacketts had a visitor — Ms Penelope Lefty, from the local Social Welfare department. Ms Lefty had very short hair bleached snow-white and a tattoo of a rose on her arm. She also wore biker boots and an earring through her eyebrow. At first the Stacketts thought she'd come to rob their house. But that wasn't why Ms Lefty was there. She wanted to know if our story was right. And once she saw that it was, things began to happen.

Meals on Wheels started turning up every day with hot food. A nurse knocked on the door, saying she'd be popping in once a week to check on both of them. The local Lions Club sent some volunteers around to build a wheelchair ramp and, while they were at it, they decided to buy the Stacketts a new electric wheelchair to go with it.

'I'm so pleased we found you,' Mrs Stackett said. 'That lovely girl Francesca wants to take our picture — all of us together. She's just gone to look for Toby.'

'Francesca?' asked Jasper. 'We don't know any Francesca.'

'That's Frankie,' I explained. 'Francesca is her real name, Frankie's just for short. And you thought she had a dumb boy's name!'

Jasper flushed. 'Francesca's a pretty name. But to tell you the truth, I'm used to calling her Frankie now. I quite like it.'

'Well, here she comes,' said old Mrs Stackett. 'Oh good, she's found Toby. Francesca! Over here, dear.'

Frankie spotted us and ran over. 'Guess what? I've just taken a picture of the Fletchers taking their little puppy for a walk — and they let me name it!'

'What did you call it?' I smiled as Frankie lined us up for a photograph. Funny, I'd never really had a best friend before. Jasper was the closest to it, and she didn't really count. But now I had Frankie.

'Tripod,' she said.

Old Mr Stackett let out a huge guffaw and slapped his leg.

The three-legged dog had been one of our most popular stories. Toby was right — people were practically stampeding over the top of each other to give it a home. But after all that, the Fletchers decided to keep him themselves.

'It was my photograph that did it, of course,' Jasper reminded us for the umpteenth time. 'How could they give him away when I made him look so cute?'

'It was a good photo,' agreed Frankie.

Jasper looked at her warily. She was still getting used to having a fourth person around.

'Thanks,' Jasper said gruffly. 'Though to be honest, I don't think I'll take any more. I'd rather write human interest stories. That's my real talent, you know.'

'What's a human interest story, dear? Is that the same thing Hugo does?' asked old Mrs Stackett.

'No way, Mrs S. A human interest story is a story about interesting humans, like you and Mr Stackett.' Jasper grinned at me. 'Hugo just writes about crooks.'

'Speaking of which,' Toby chimed in. 'I wonder if Mayor Fitzherbert is here today?'

'*Mister* Fitzherbert,' I corrected him. 'Don't forget he's not the Mayor any more. And I doubt he's here. He's probably out looking for a job.'

Yep, things had really changed since the day that *Street Wise* came out one month ago. That Tuesday night, so many residents turned up to the council meeting after reading our story that it was standing room only in the public gallery. Jasper and I couldn't go because we were still grounded but Toby told us what happened.

As we suspected, nobody wanted the park turned into a big fancy high-rise tower for rich people. As soon as the Mayor suggested it, there was pandemonium. After all, as Mayor he was supposed to do the right thing for everybody — not try to trick them into something they didn't want. Nobody likes that! People booed and jeered and stamped their feet. There was so much noise the councillors closed the meeting and called the police to break it up.

Needless to say, Barry Plunder's plan didn't go through. The next day the Mayor resigned and, when the local paper tried to contact Barry Plunder, his receptionist said he'd gone to the Bahamas for a very long holiday. So they put us on the front page instead. Once that happened, Mum and Dad *had* to forgive us.

'I wonder what Howard Fitzherbert is doing today?' mused Toby. 'You know, I feel quite sorry for him, after everything that happened.'

'I don't,' snapped Jasper. 'It serves him right for putting that virus into Myron.'

That was another mystery solved. When the police turned up at the Fitzherbert mansion to ask the Mayor a few questions about the riot at the council chambers, Howard thought they'd come to arrest *him*. It was his guilty conscience that got him. He started bawling his eyes out and begging the cops not to take him away. The funny thing is, it wasn't the newspaper he was trying to destroy. He didn't care about that. He just wanted to wreck Toby's computer before school started again.

Howard knew darn well that spreading computer viruses is a crime. But when the police asked Toby if he wanted to press charges, he said no. He thought Howard had enough punishment coming already because of his dad's disgrace. But Howard ended up being punished anyway. His mother said Howard needed to be 'disciplined', so while the rest of us were enjoying Blue Rock's first annual Party in the Park, Howard was doing time at Sergeant Butch Hardknuckle's Camp for Boys.

'Howard's probably hanging off a fifty metre cliff or fighting off crocodiles,' I said.

Jasper looked quite happy at the thought of it. Then she said, 'Gosh, doesn't the park look better now all that barbed wire's gone?'

We gazed around us. The new Mayor had wasted no time. With so many angry residents protesting against the council, she knew she had to do something quick smart. Within two days, the fence had been torn down, the old car wrecks had been towed away, and a whole team of gardeners was busy planting trees and flowers. A wooden sign saying 'The Village Green' went up over the front gate.

'And not before time,' said Great-aunt Miranda approvingly. 'The new Mayor might not be so bad after all.'

Then, the new Mayor announced a big party to celebrate the park reopening — and everyone in Blue Rock was invited.

'They've even fixed the skate ramp.' It seemed like years since I had fallen off and cracked my head. 'Remember the day you tripped me, Jasper?'

Jasper tossed her head. 'Lucky for us I did. We wouldn't have made the newspaper if I hadn't.'

'And I wouldn't have my new electric hot-rod!' crowed old Mr Stackett, doing another wheelie.

'I wouldn't be a professional photographer like my dad!' added Frankie.

'And don't forget the most important thing,' Toby reminded us. 'If it wasn't for your accident, Hugo, Blue Rock wouldn't have got its park back.'

Standing there under the old fig tree, I must admit

I felt pretty lucky. But as the bush band struck up another song, a wave of sadness washed over me. So much had happened while we were writing the newspaper — and now it was all over.

'Do you think we'll ever do it again?' I asked. 'Another issue of *Street Wise*?'

Nobody said a word. I knew they were all feeling the same way.

Mr Stackett's bright eyes looked searchingly at each of us in turn. Suddenly, he broke out into a loud cackle.

'Do fish swim?' He turned his wheelchair around and roared off towards the crowd. 'Come on kids — let's party.'

The Newspaper Kids 2

✱ Mandy Miami and the Miracle Motel

by Juanita Phillips

War has been declared!
Howard Fitzherbert has started his own
newspaper to try and run the newspaper kids
out of business! He's stealing all their ideas.
They need a special front page story. Toby's
favourite singer, Mandy Miami, could be
exactly what they want, but Mandy is so
mysterious, even her fan club don't know
how to find her. The World Wide Web holds
the clues but the newspaper kids aren't the
only ones surfing the Net – so is the Shark.

If a story breaks, the newspaper kids are
on the case!

The Newspaper Kids 3

✳ Pegleg Paddy's Puppy Factory

by Juanita Phillips

Jasper and Hugo are trapped at Auntie
Marge's Fun Camp for Kids – but the only
ones having fun are mean old Auntie Marge
and her no-good son, Pegleg Paddy. Their
creepy old house is full of strange goings-on
that have the newspaper kids' noses
twitching. With the help of a little lost dog,
they are soon on the trail of the biggest dog-
gone story their newspaper has ever
published.

If a story breaks, the newspaper kids are
on the case!

The Newspaper Kids 4

✱ Spooking Sally

by Juanita Phillips

Sally Champion is not afraid of anything!
She's not scared of ghosts or graveyards or
even Bonecrusher, the meanest dog in town.
So the newspaper kids have come up with the
biggest dare 'n' scare competition that Blue
Rock has ever seen – the *Street Wise*
Spooking Sally Challenge! The only problem
is, Sally really is hard to spook. But when
some rare dinosaur bones go missing, the
scene is set to scare Sally out of her skin!

If a story breaks, the newspaper kids are
on the case!

The Sleepover Club at Felicity's

Join the Sleepover Club: Frankie, Kenny, Felicity, Rosie and Lyndsey, five girls who just want to have fun – but who always end up in mischief.

A sleepover isn't a sleepover without a midnight feast and when the food runs out and everyone's still hungry, the Sleepover Club tiptoe down to the kitchen. But – quick! – the toaster's on fire!

Pack up your sleepover kit and drop in on the fun!

0 00 675236 5
£2. 99

Order Form

To order direct from the publishers, just make a list of the titles you want and fill in the form below:

Name ....

Address ....

....

....

Send to: Dept 6, HarperCollins Publishers Ltd, Westerhill Road, Bishopbriggs, Glasgow G64 2QT.

Please enclose a cheque or postal order to the value of the cover price, plus:

UK & BFPO: Add £1.00 for the first book, and 25p per copy for each additional book ordered.

Overseas and Eire: Add £2.95 service charge. Books will be sent by surface mail but quotes for airmail despatch will be given on request.

A 24-hour telephone ordering service is available to holders of Visa, MasterCard, Amex or Switch cards on 0141- 772 2281.

Collins
An *Imprint of* HarperCollins*Publishers*